MW00955162

Dear Parents and Caregivers,

If your child is ready to learn how to read, then you've come to the right place! We want kids to reach for the stars as they begin their reading adventure. With Ready-to-Go!, this very first level has been carefully mapped out to launch their reading voyage.

All books in this level share the following:

★ **Just the right length:** each story has about 100 words, many of them repeated.

★ **Sight words:** frequently used words that children will come to recognize by sight, such as "the" and "can."

★ **Word families:** rhyming words used throughout the story for ease of recognition.

★ **A guide at the beginning** that prompts children to sound out the words before they start reading.

★ **Questions at the end** for children to re-engage with the story.

★ **Fun stories** starring children's favorite characters so learning to read is a blast.

These books will provide children with confidence in their reading abilities as they go from mastering the letters of the alphabet to understanding how those letters create words, sentences, and stories.

Blast off on this starry adventure . . . a universe of reading awaits!

BATMAN™ HAS A PLAN

By Tina Gallo

Illustrated by Patrick Spaziante

Batman created by Bob Kane with Bill Finger

Ready-to-Read

Simon Spotlight

New York   London   Toronto   Sydney   New Delhi

Here is a list of all the words you will find in this book. Sound them out before you begin reading the story.

Names:

Batman

The Penguin

Copyright © 2018 DC Comics. BATMAN and all related characters and elements © & ™
DC Comics & Warner Bros. Entertainment Inc. (s18)

SIMON SPOTLIGHT

An imprint of Simon & Schuster Children's Publishing Division
1230 Avenue of the Americas, New York, New York 10020 • This Simon Spotlight edition May 2018
All rights reserved, including the right of reproduction in whole or in part in any form.
SIMON SPOTLIGHT, READY-TO-READ, and colophon are registered trademarks of Simon & Schuster, Inc.
For information about special discounts for bulk purchases, please contact Simon & Schuster Special Sales at
1-866-506-1949 or business@simonandschuster.com. Manufactured in the United States of America 0318 LAK
1 2 3 4 5 6 7 8 9 10 ISBN 978-1-5344-1639-0 (hc) ISBN 978-1-5344-1638-3 (pbk) ISBN 978-1-5344-1640-6 (eBook)

Word families:

"-an"	→	can	plan	
"-ack"	→	back	black	sack
"-all"	→	fall	wall	
"-ad"	→	mad	glad	

Sight words:

a	and	but	down	go
has	how	in	is	not
take	thank	the	there	this
up	will	you		

Bonus words:

everyone	money	

Ready to go? Happy reading!

Don't miss the questions about the story
on the last page of this book.

This is Batman.

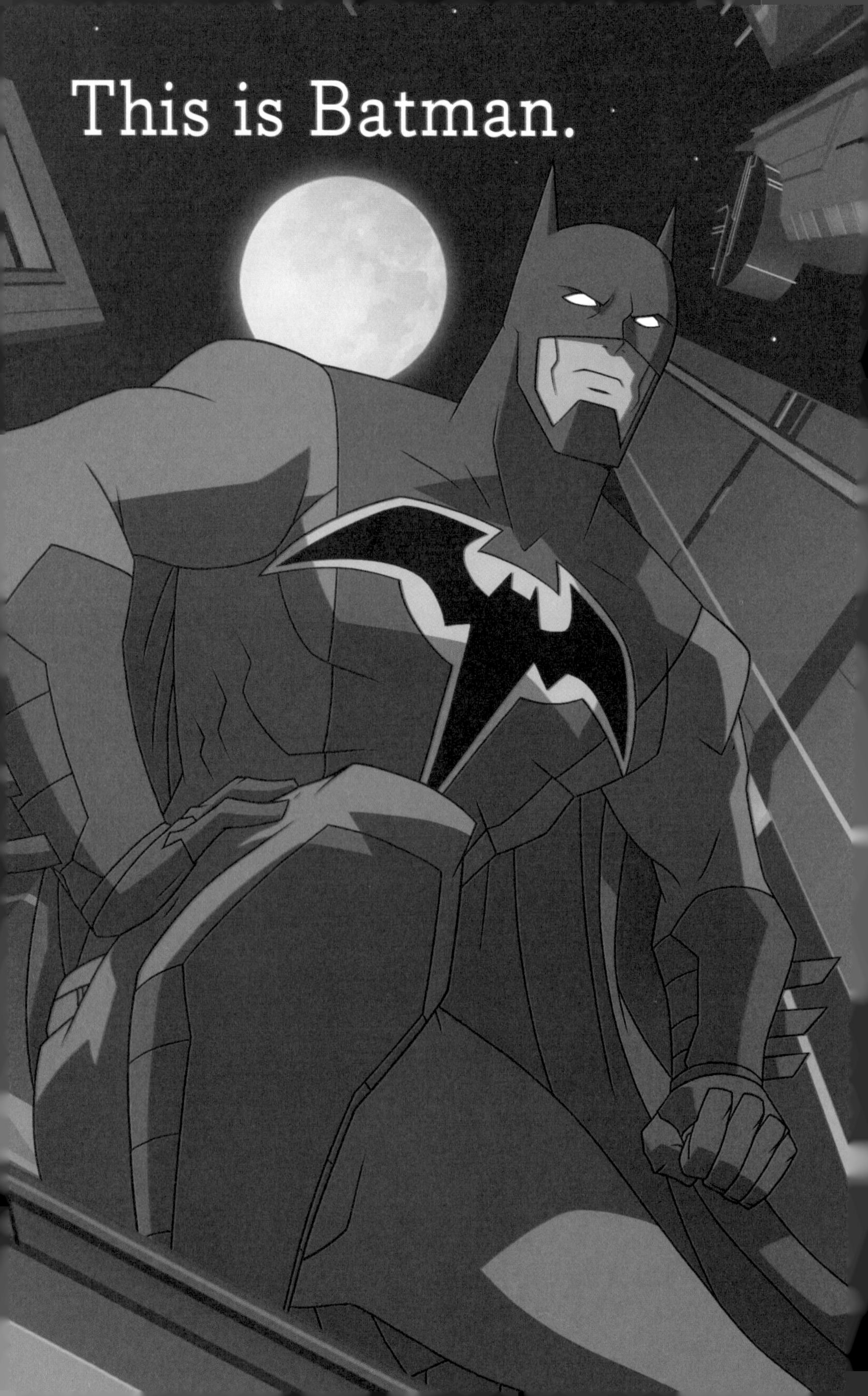

This is the Penguin.

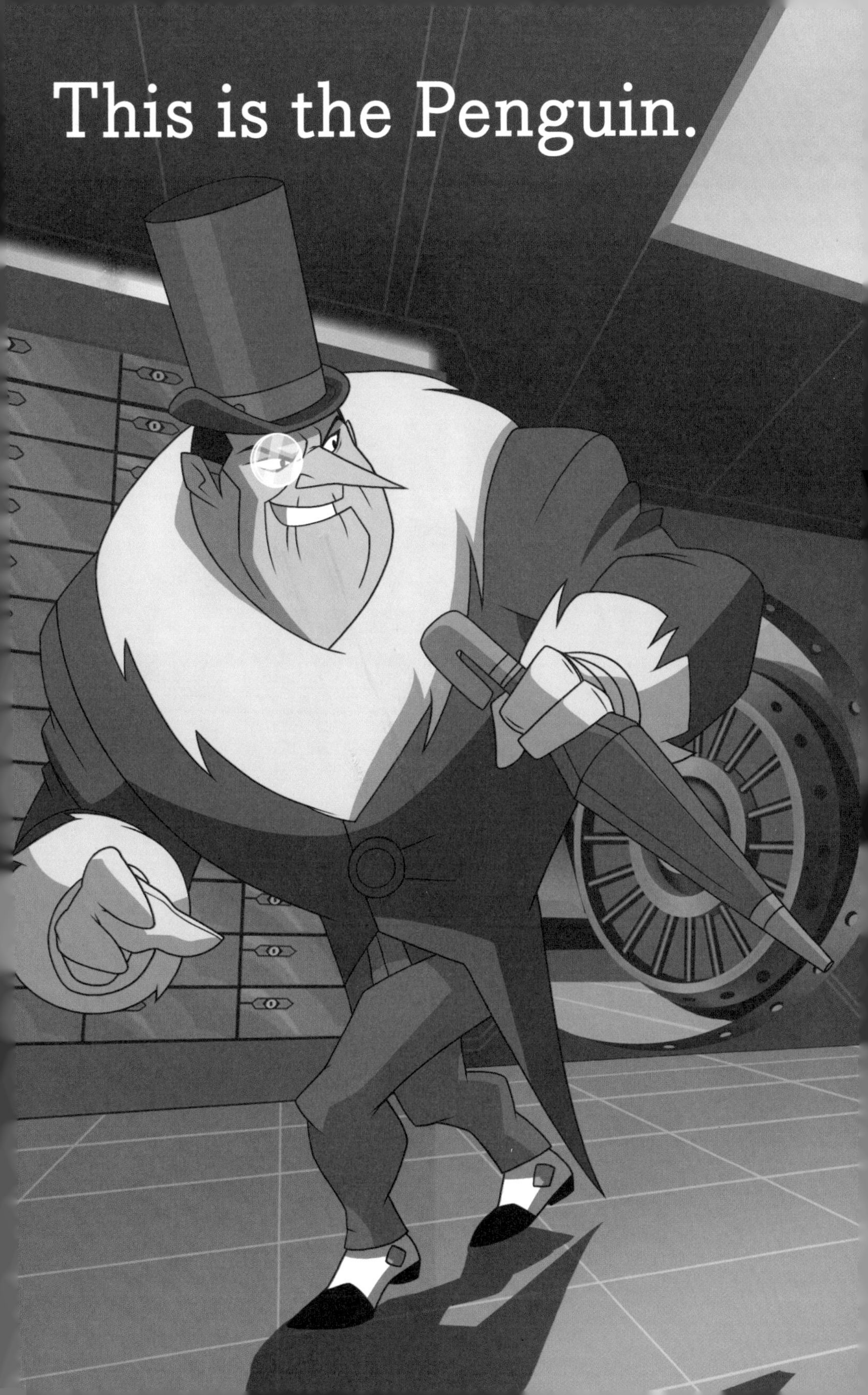

This is the money.

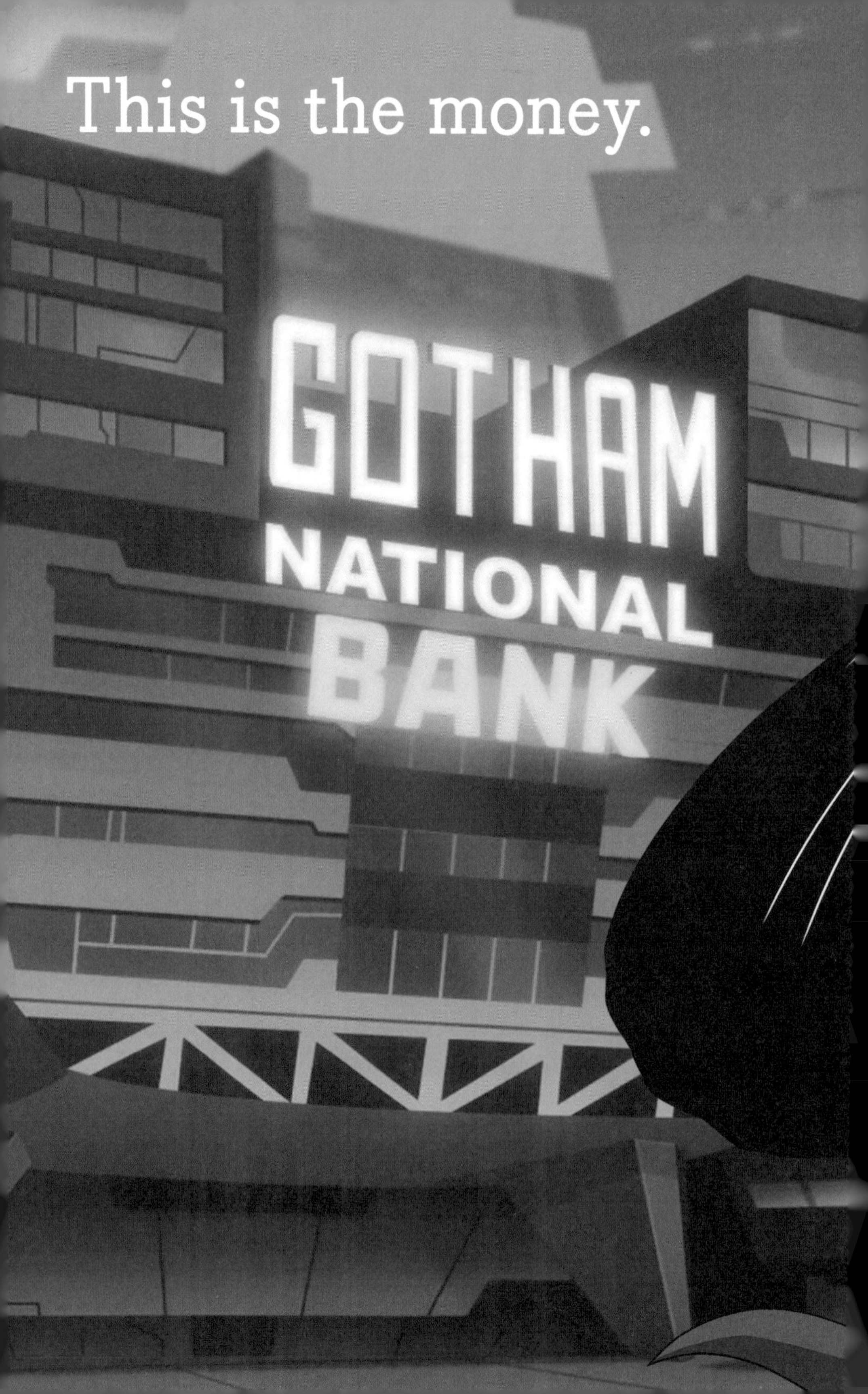
GOTHAM
NATIONAL
BANK

The money is in a black sack.

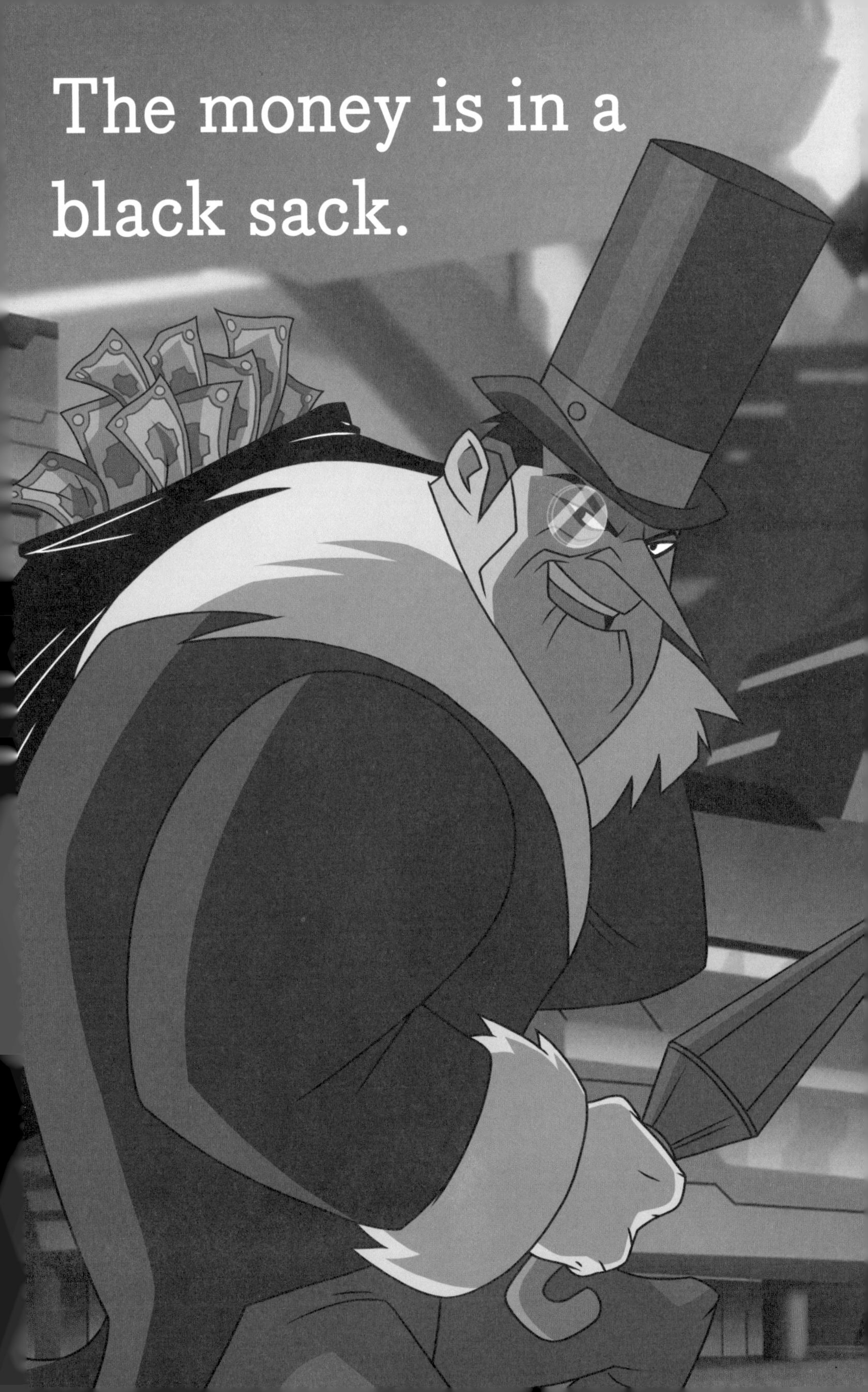

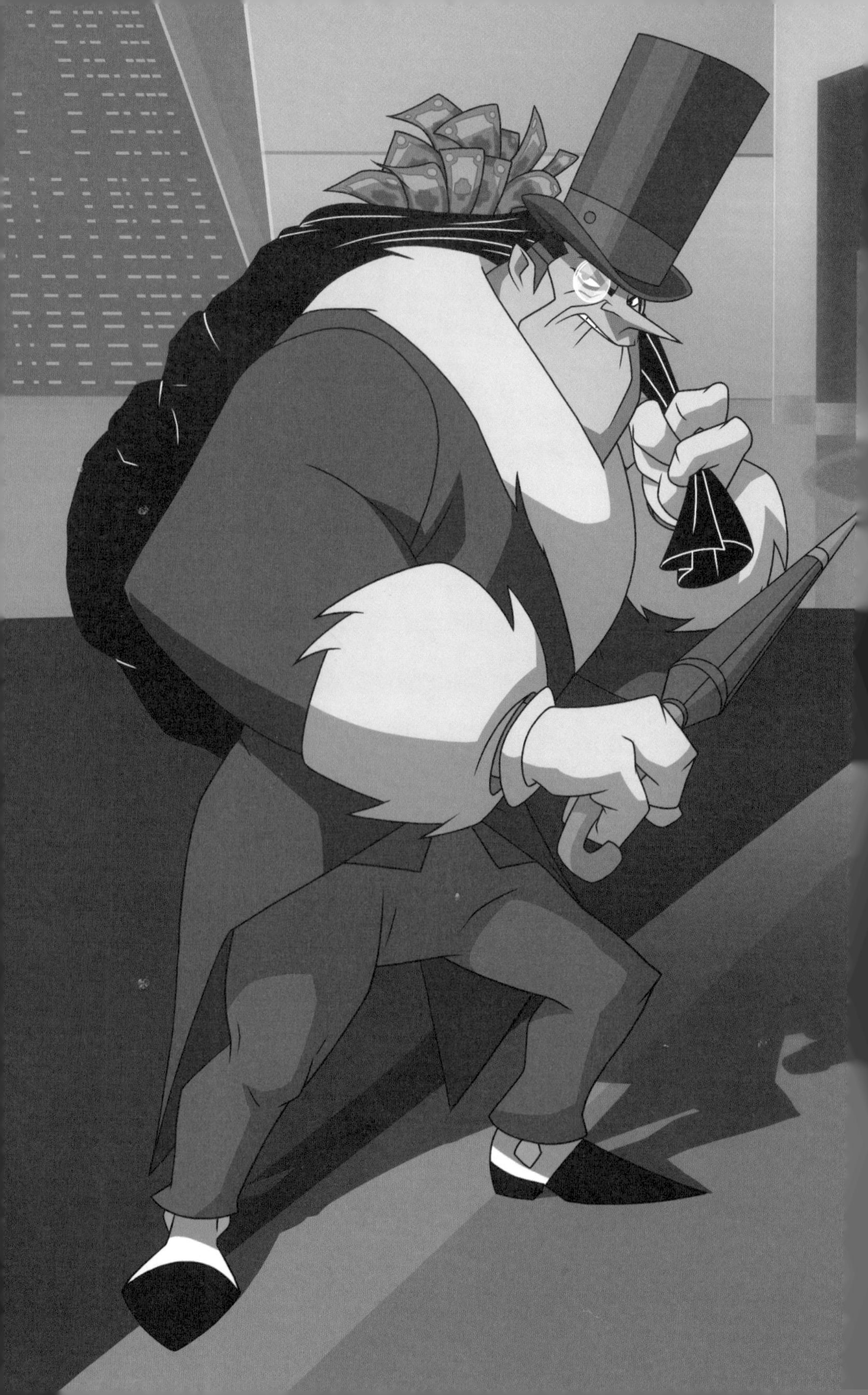

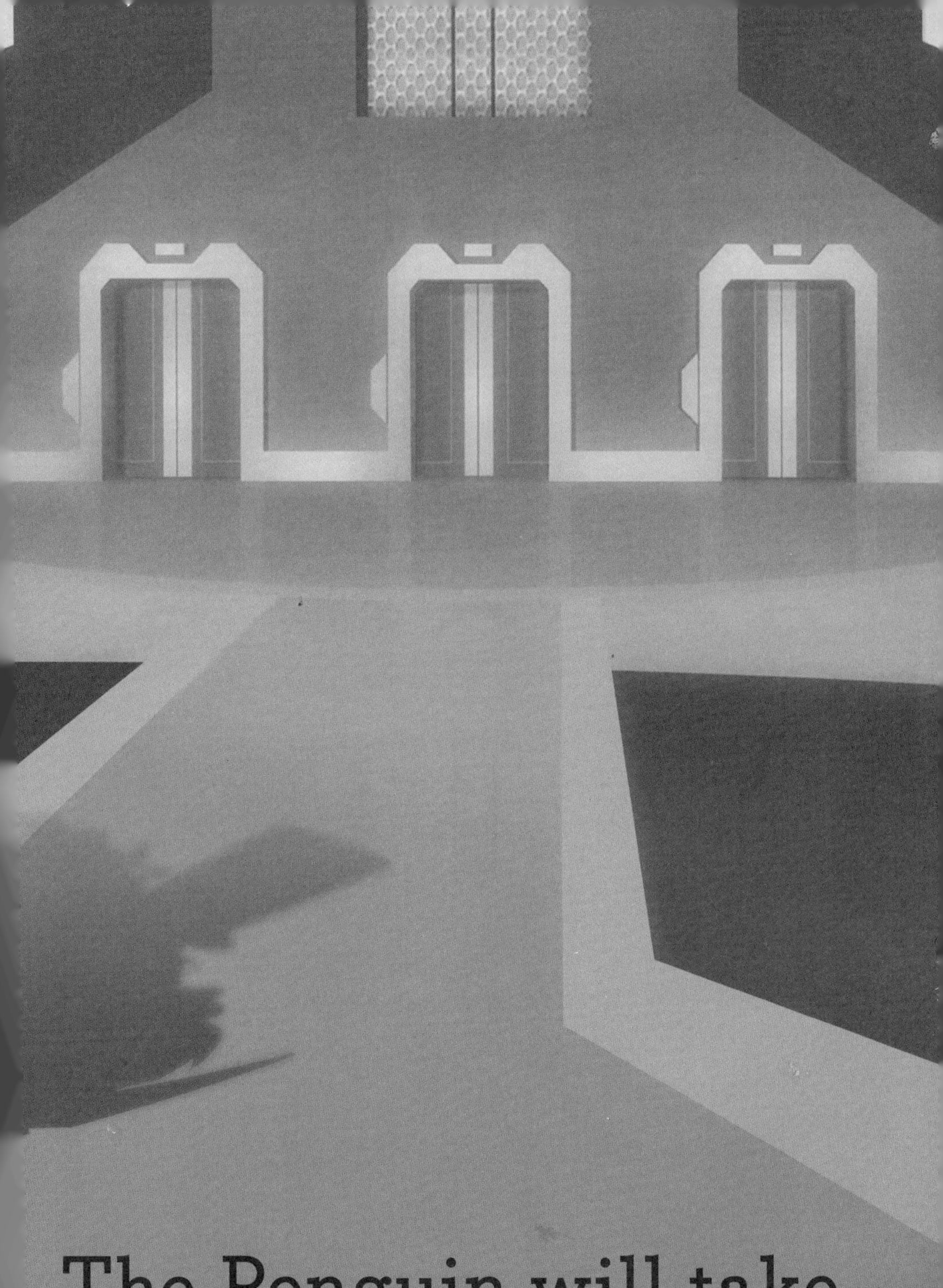

The Penguin will take the money.

Batman will take the money back.

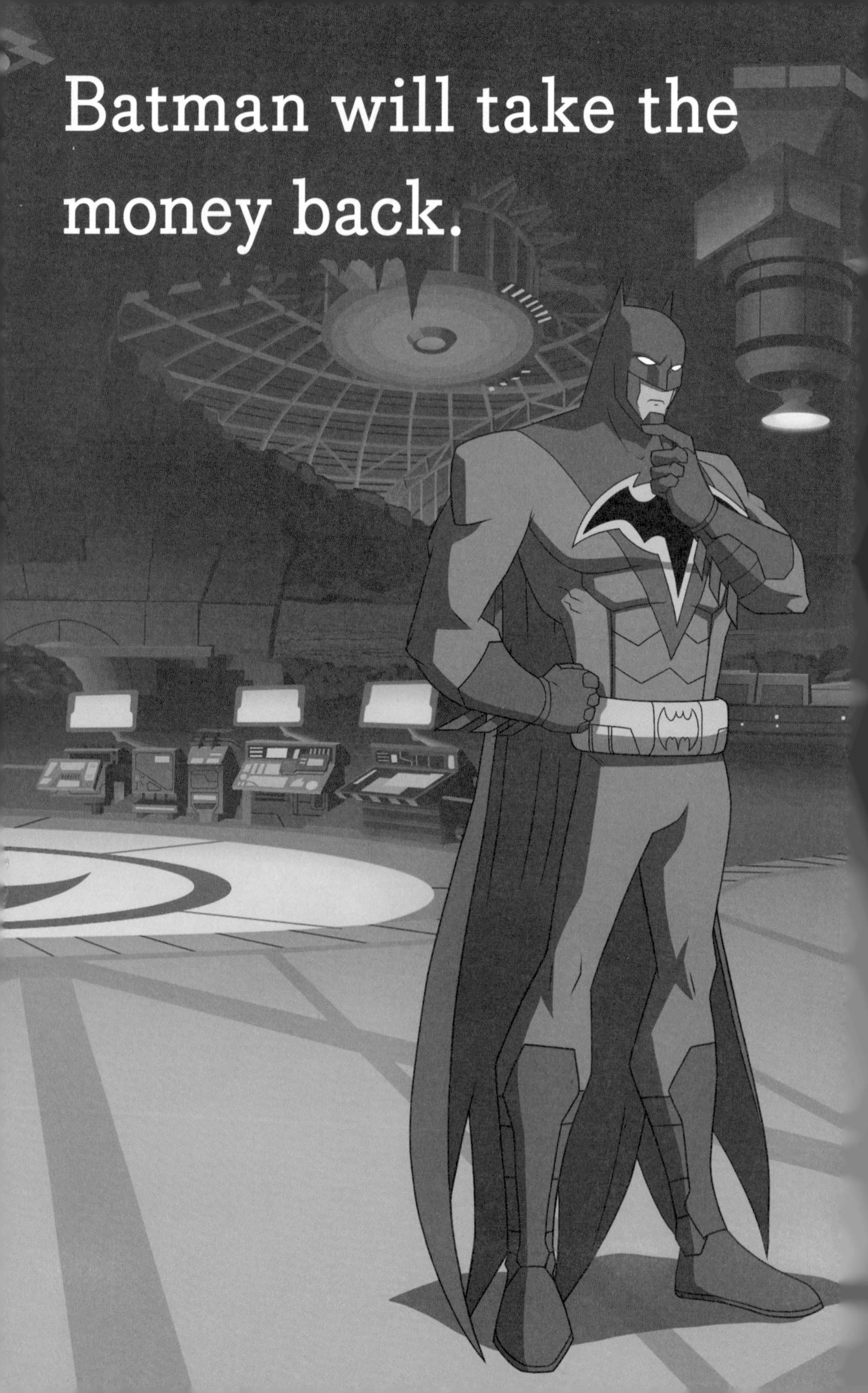

But how?

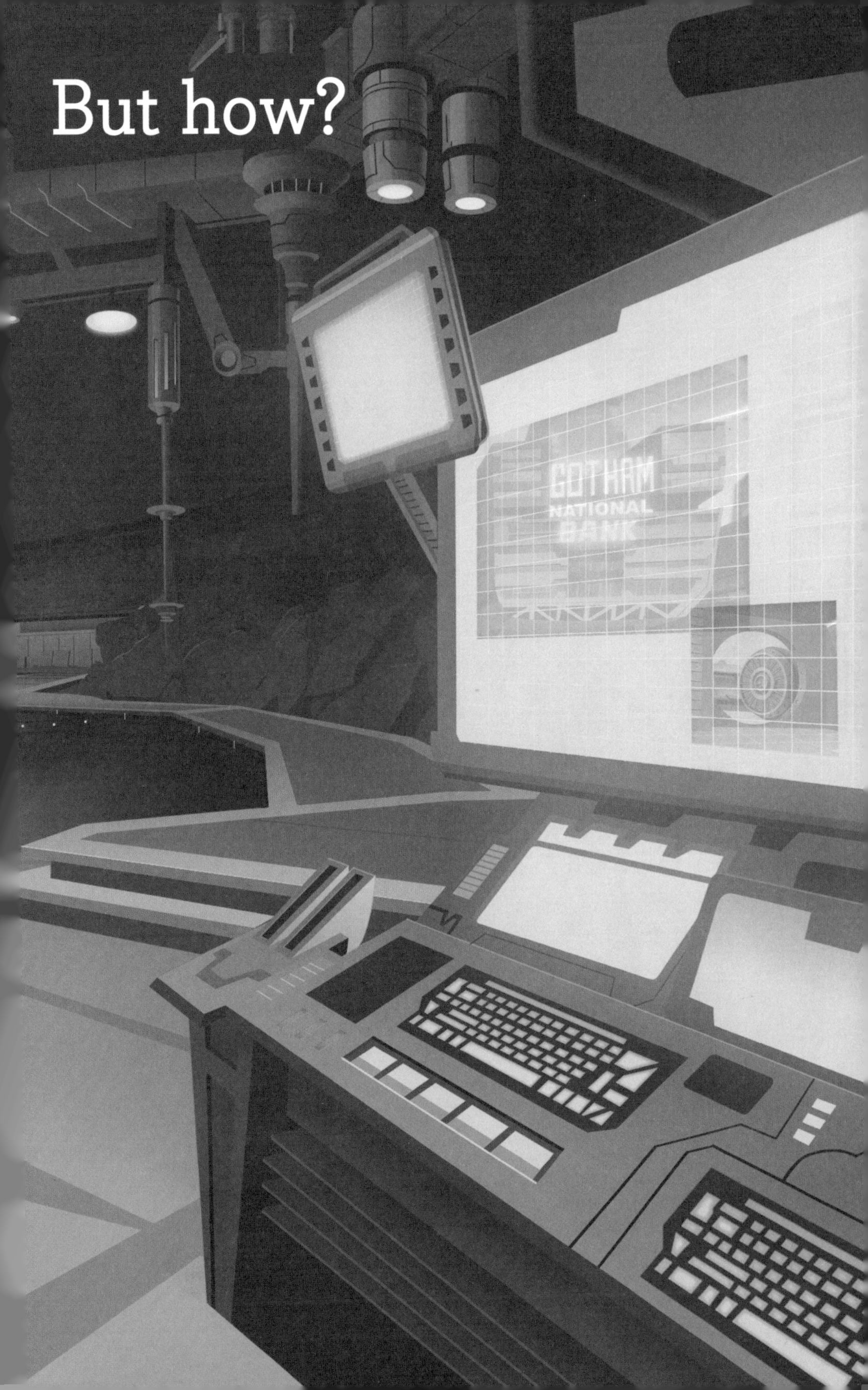
GOTHAM
NATIONAL
BANK

Batman has a plan.

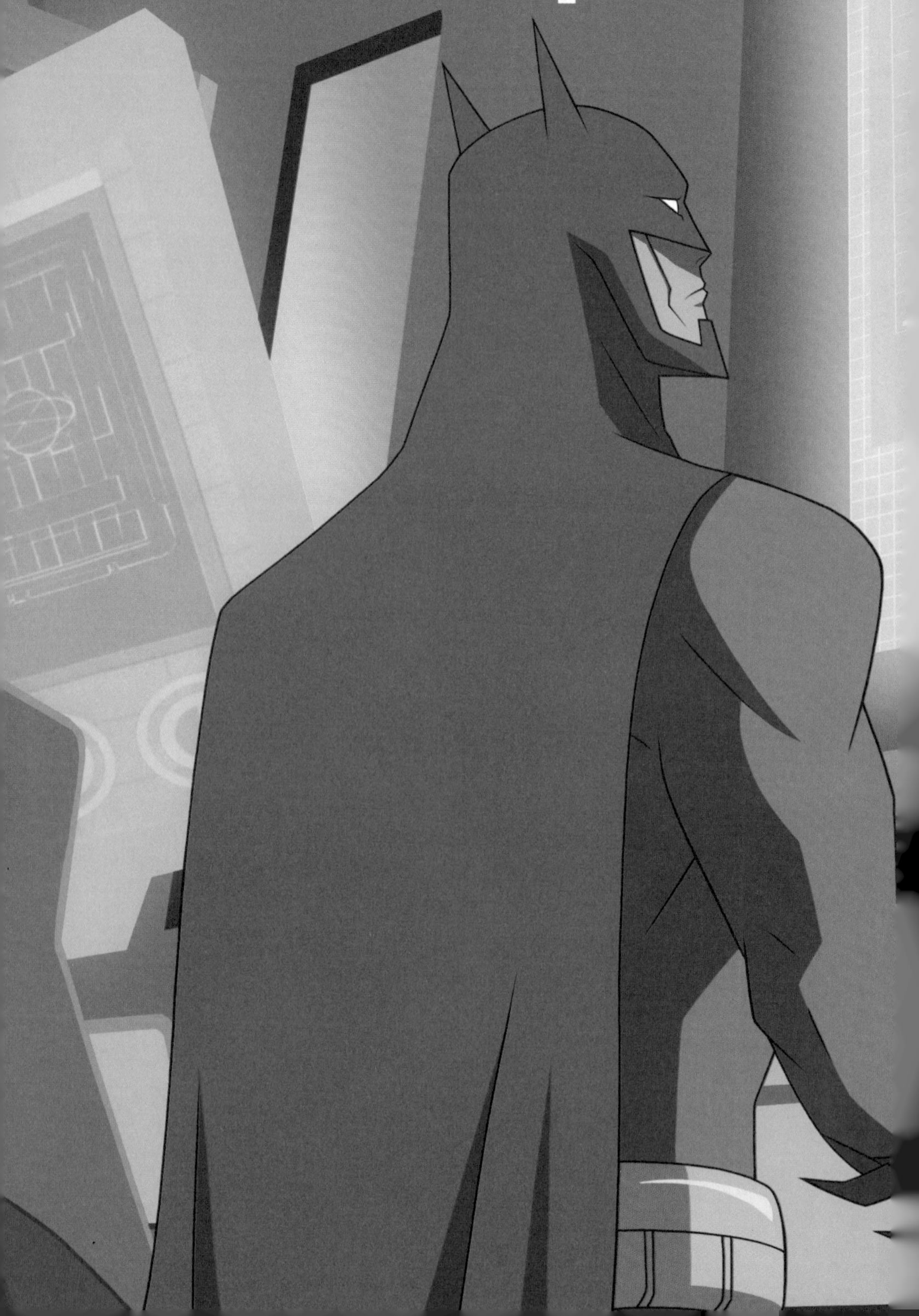

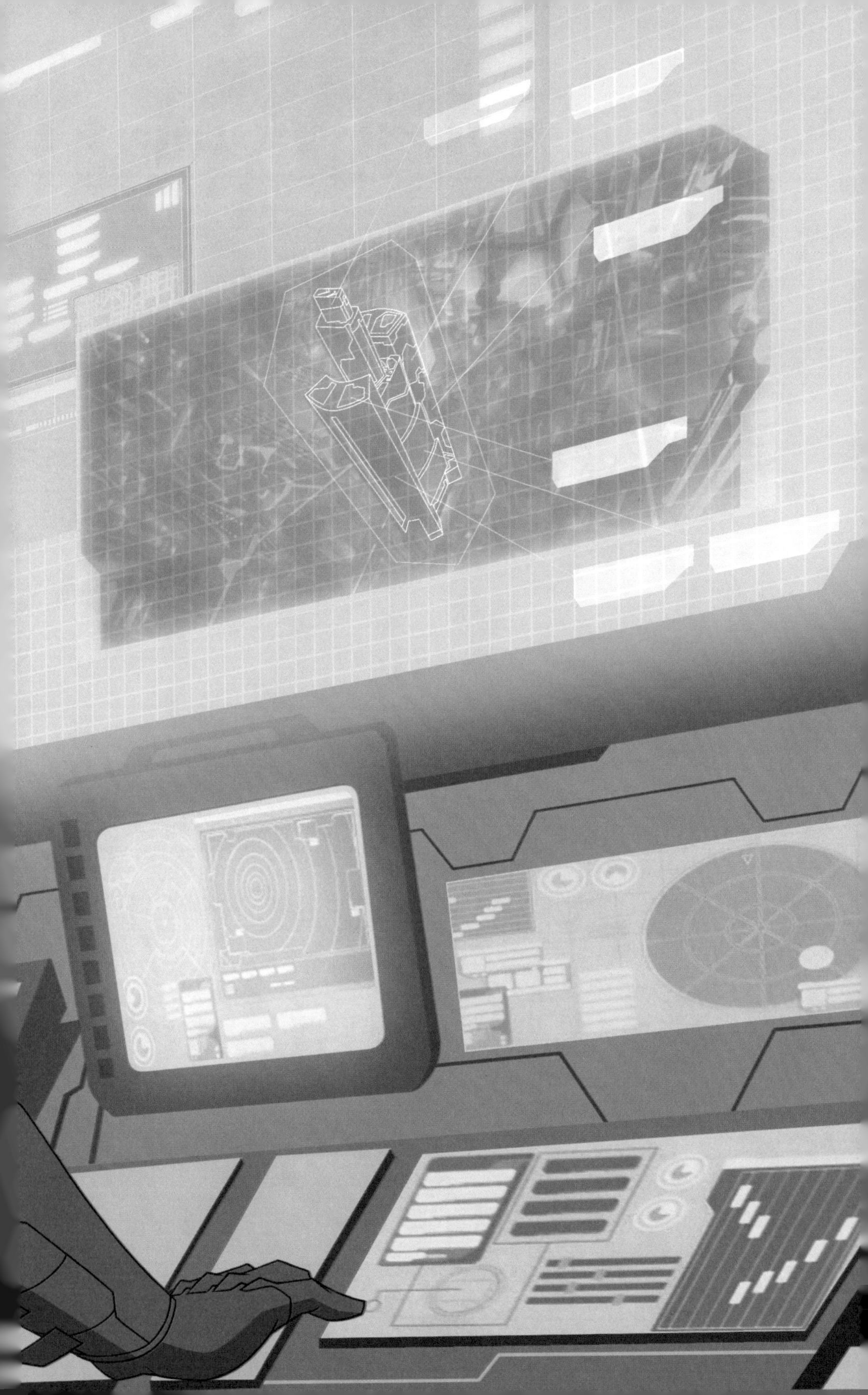

Batman can go up.

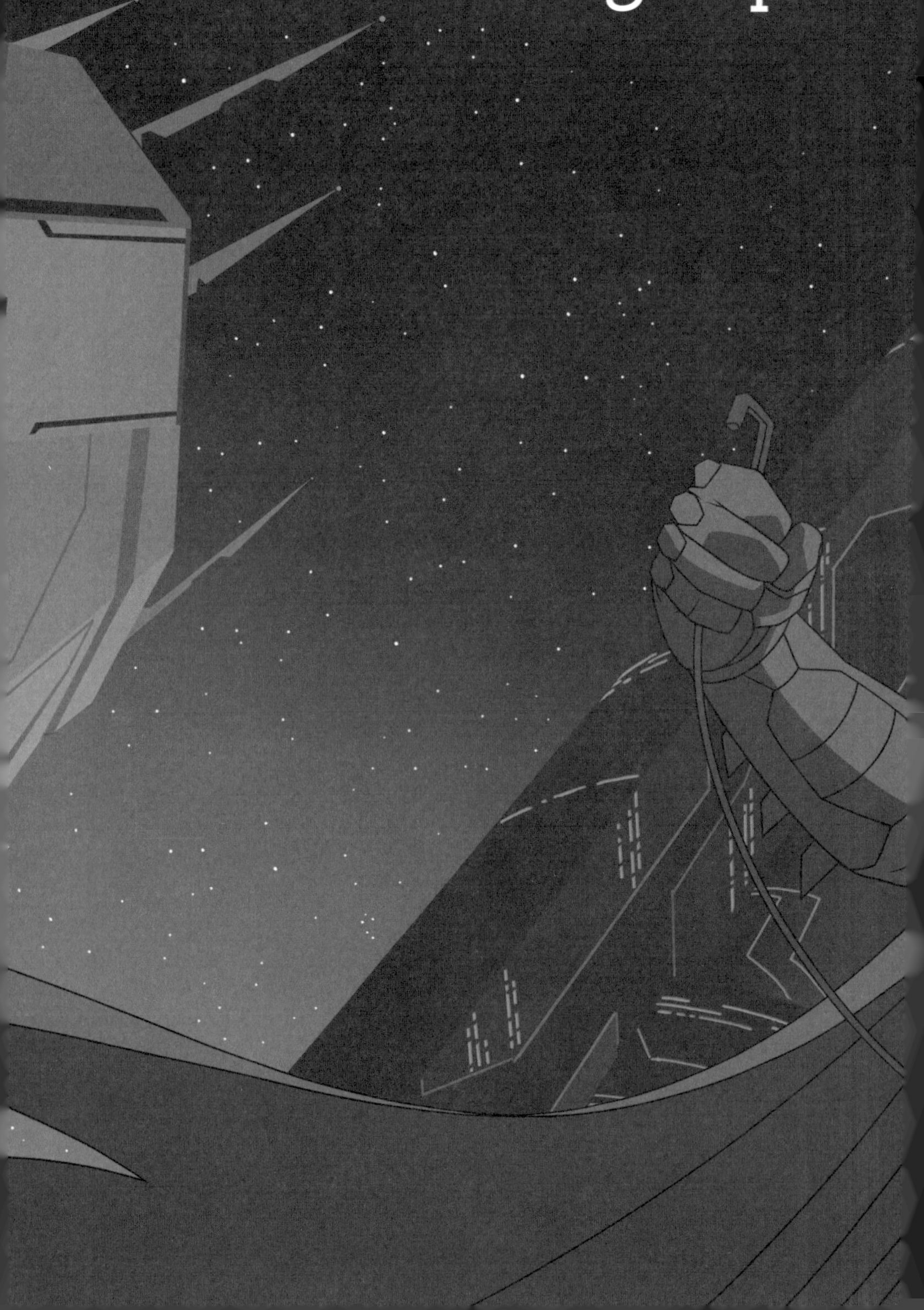

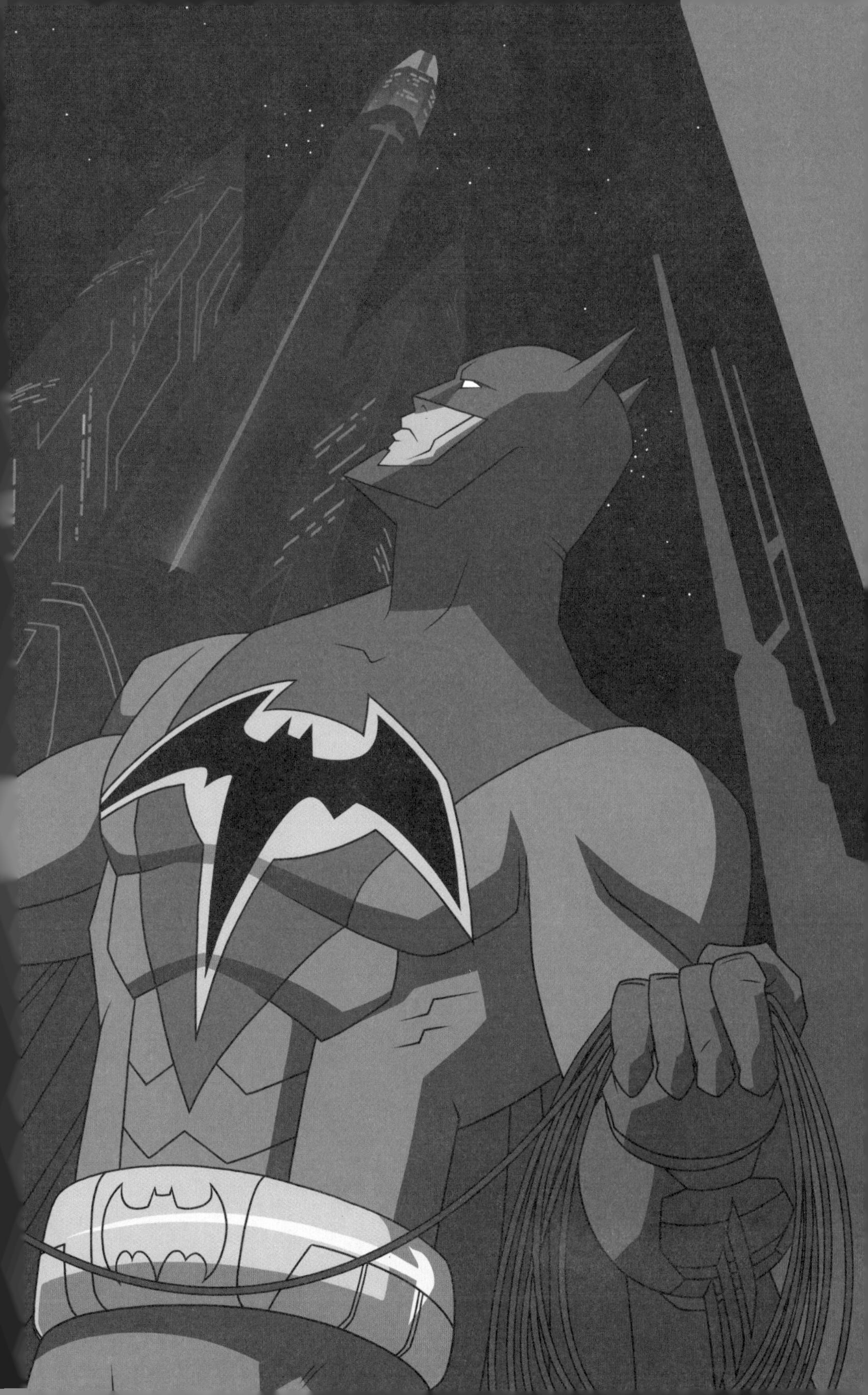

Batman can go up the wall.

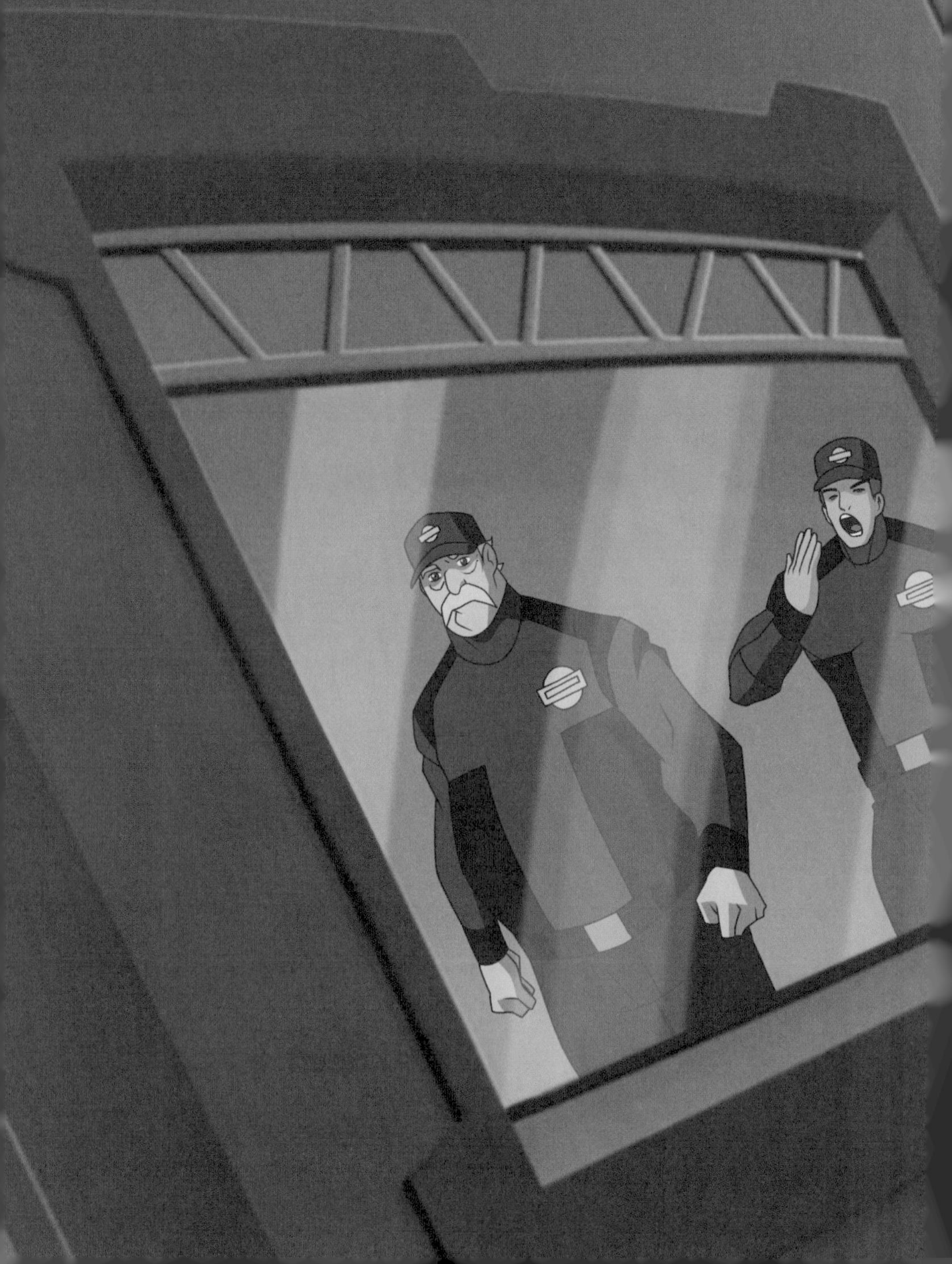

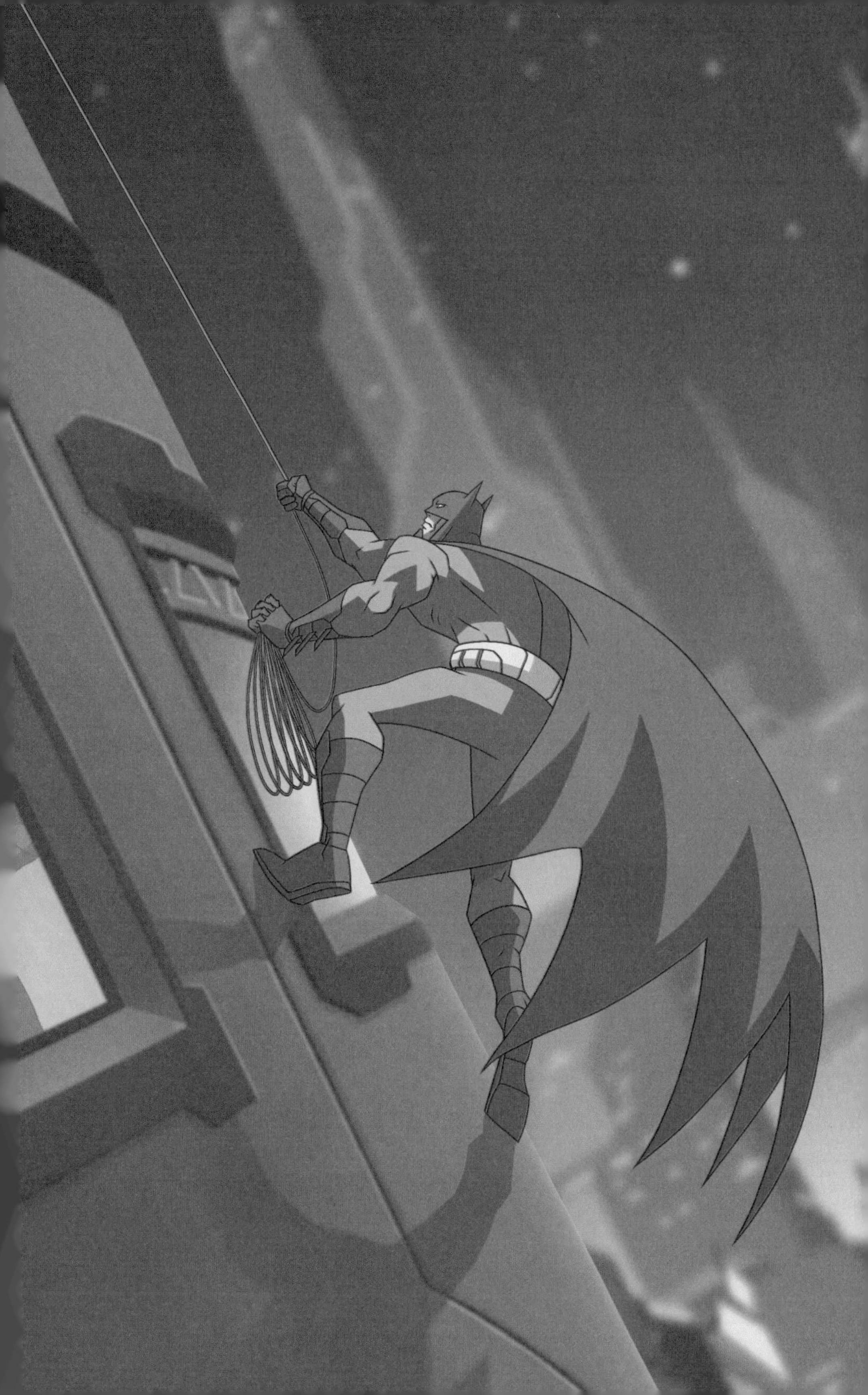

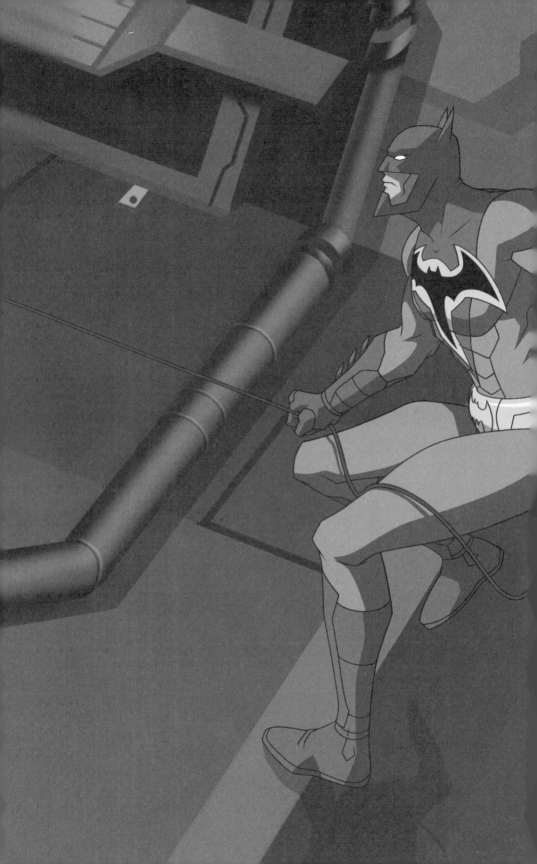

Batman will not fall.

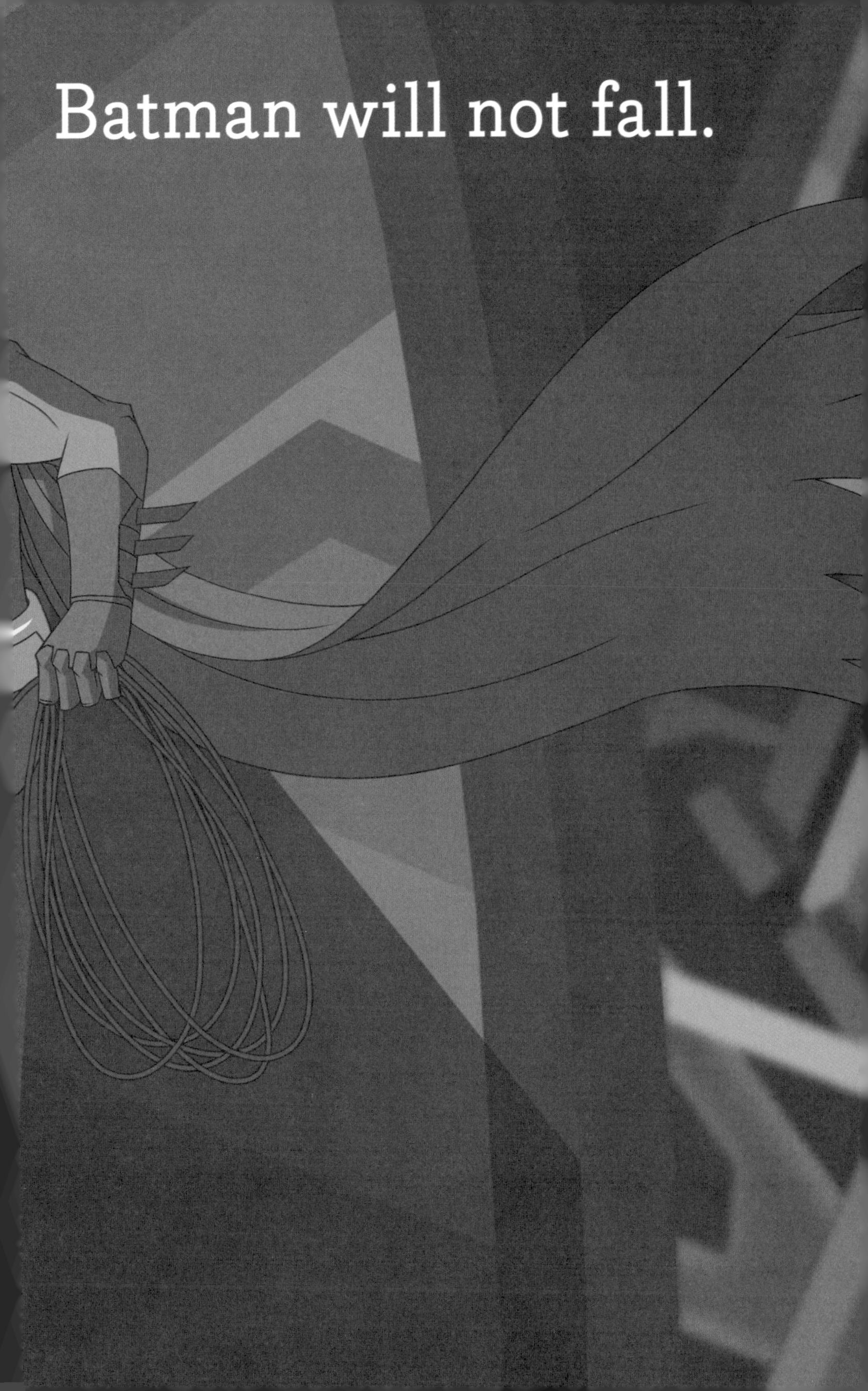

There is the money!

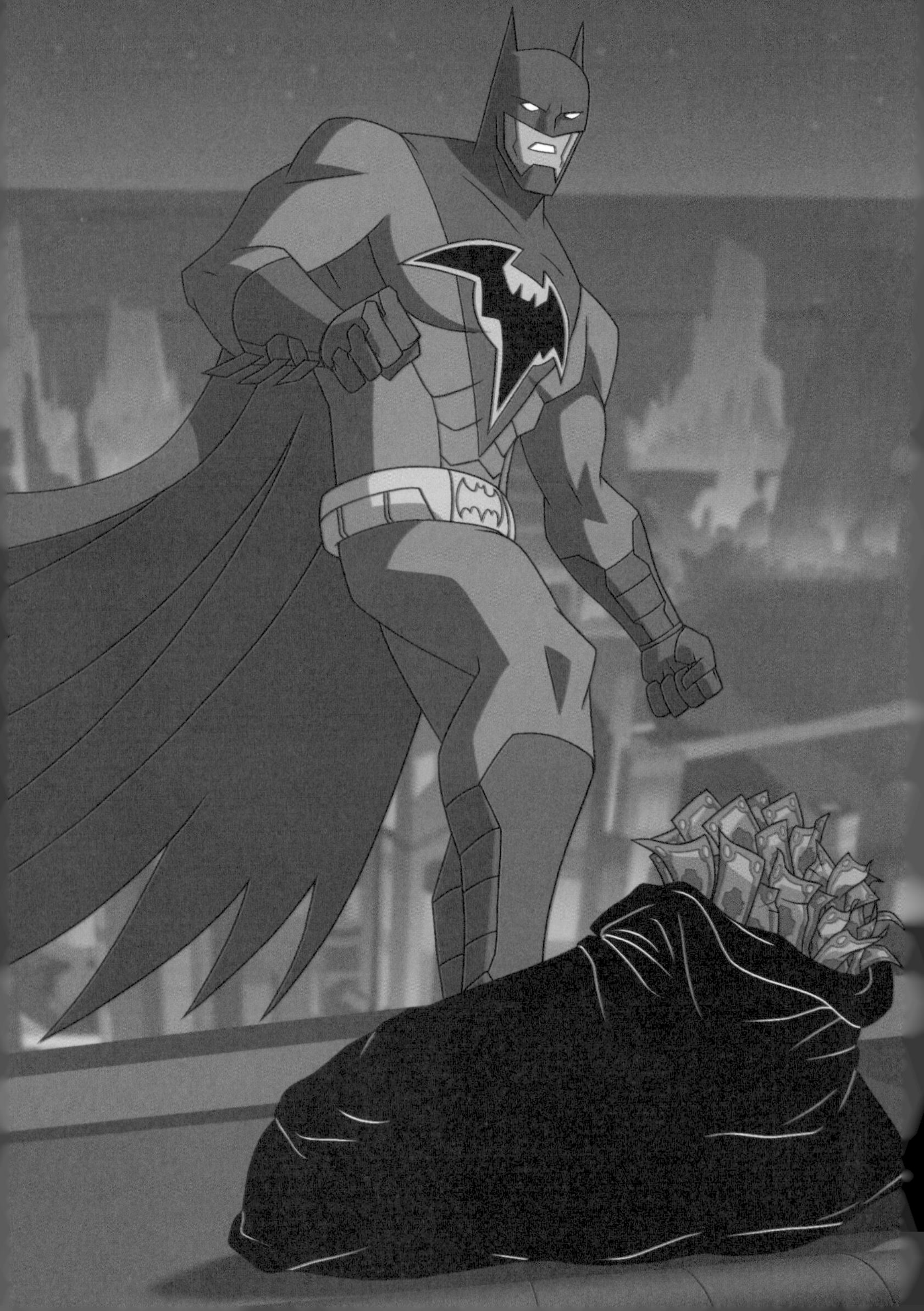

Batman has the money.

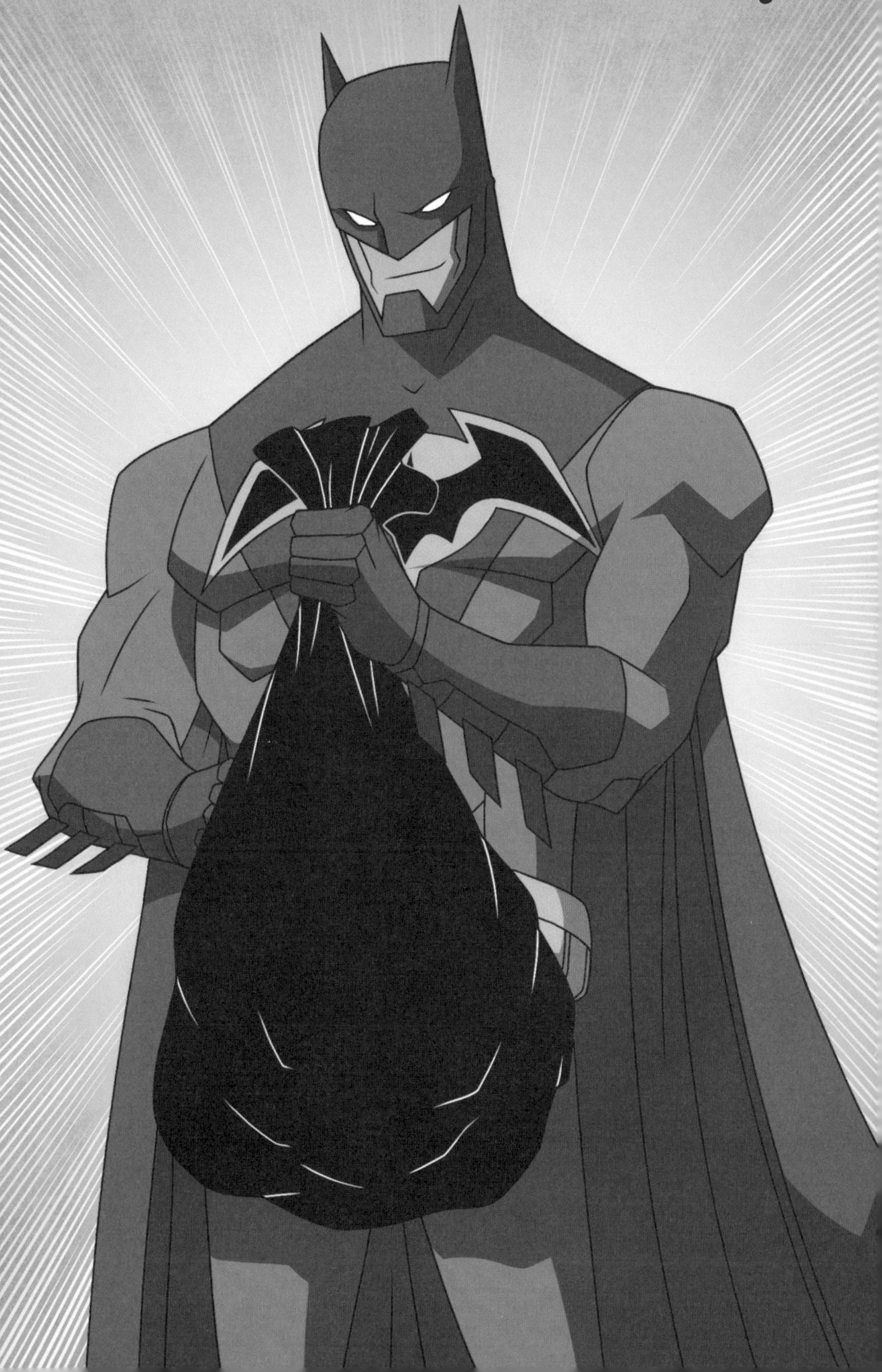

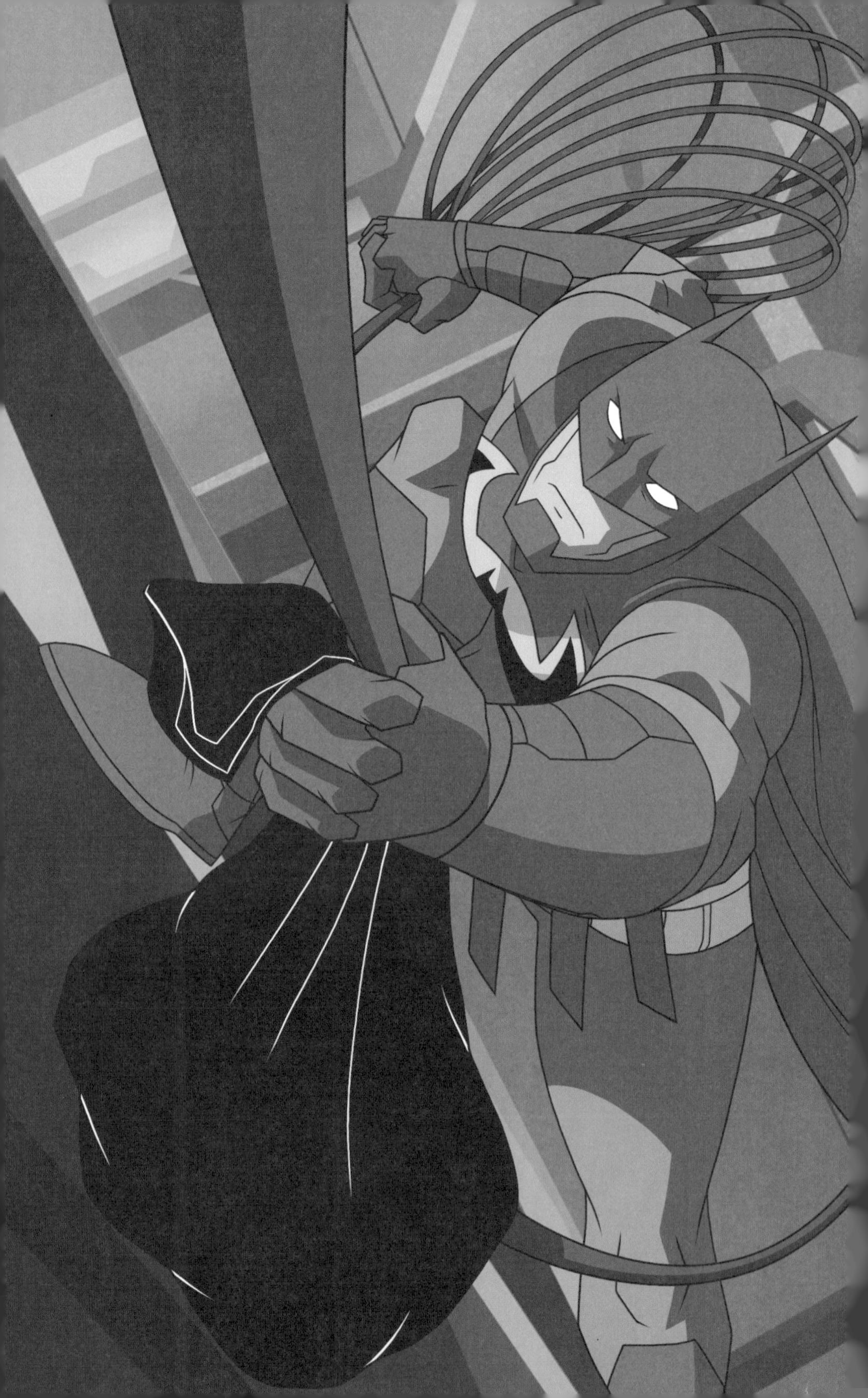

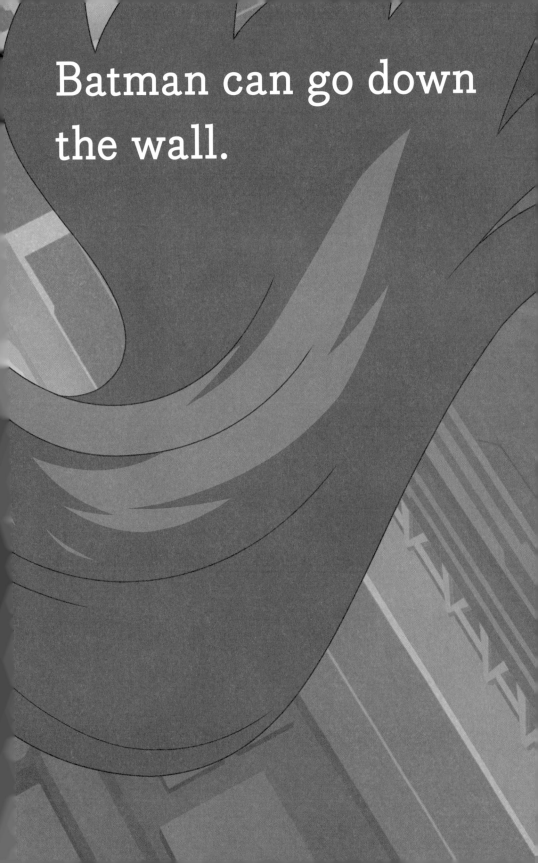

Batman can go down
the wall.

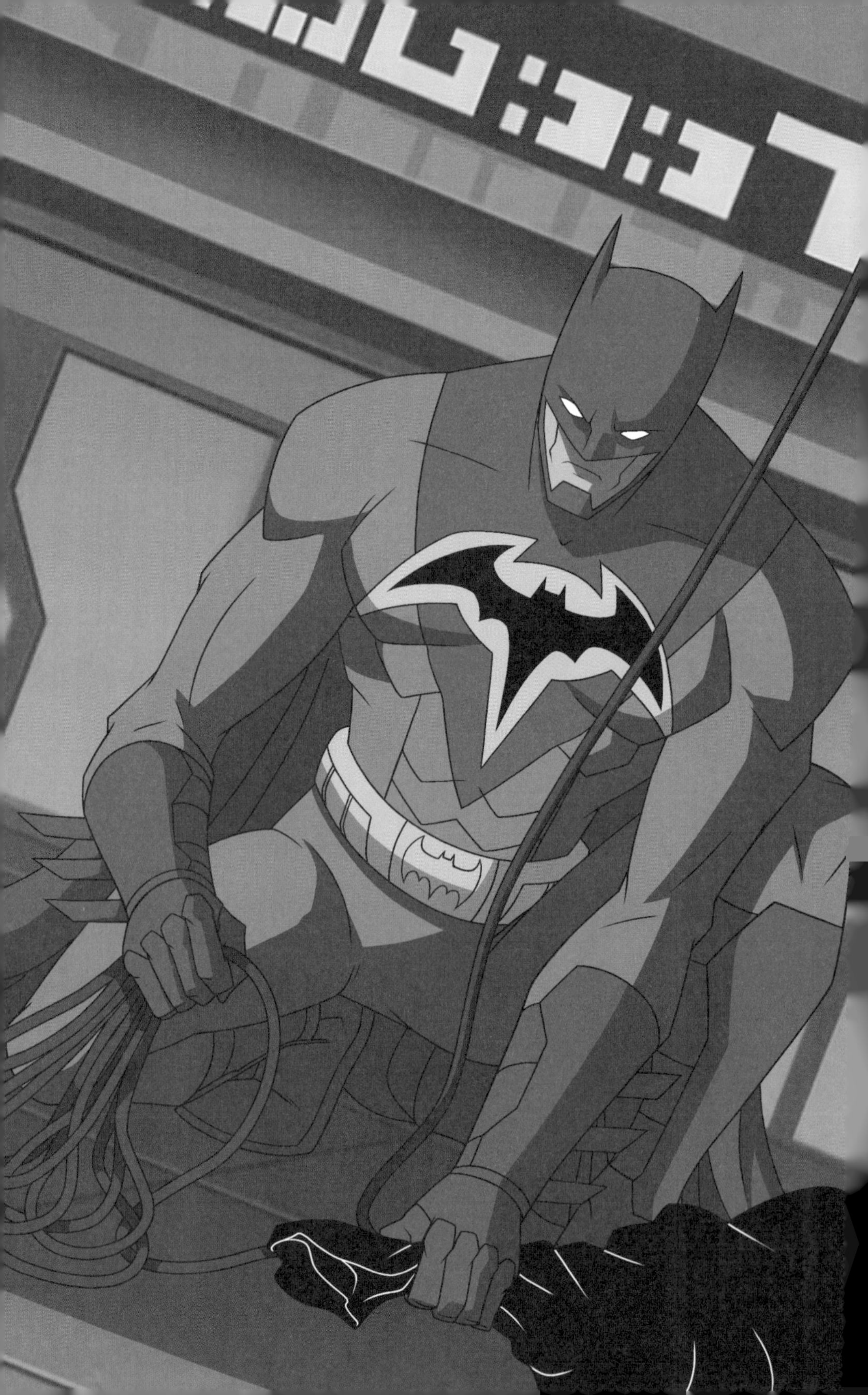

There is the Penguin!

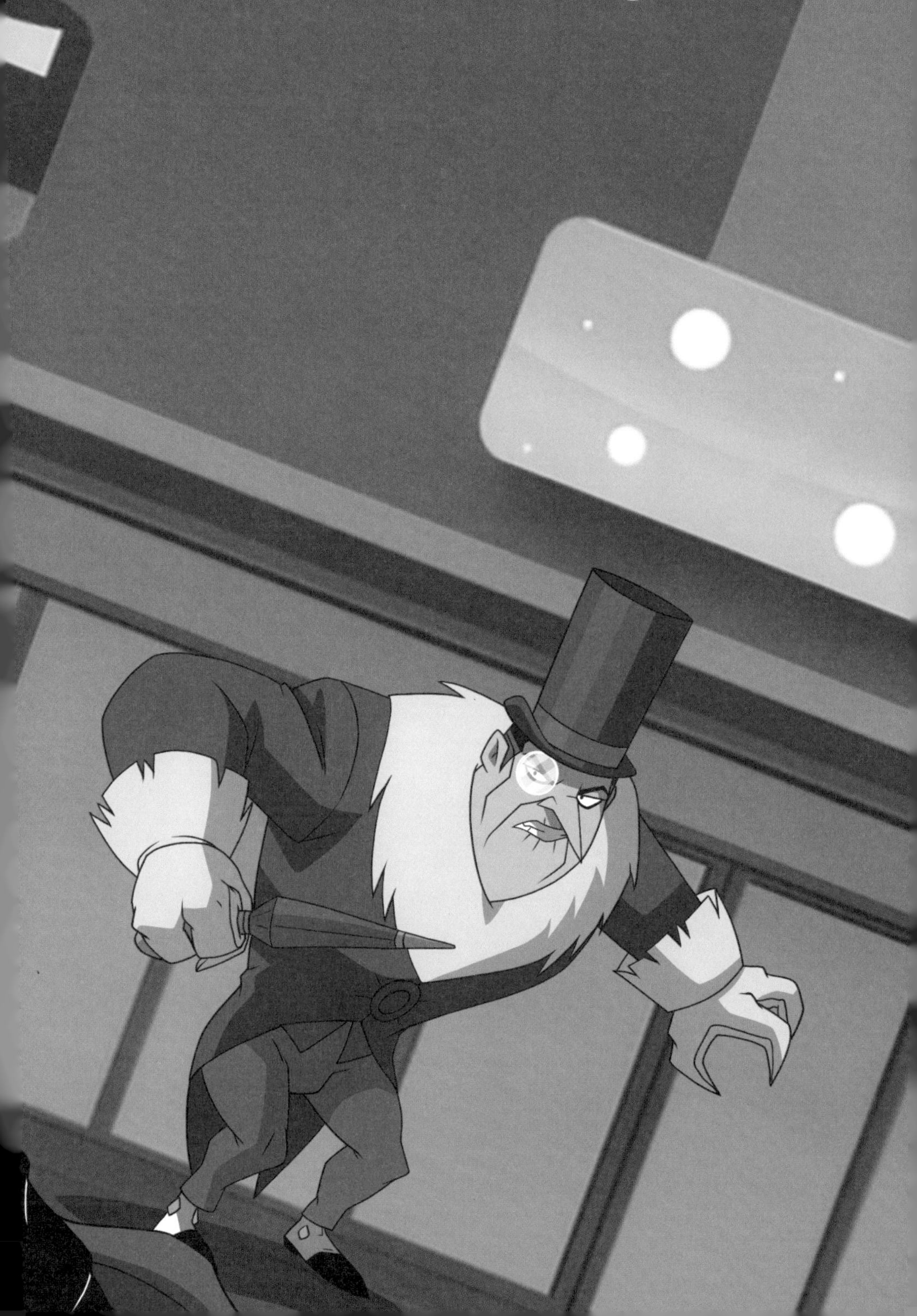

Batman has a plan.
Batman has the money
and the Penguin!

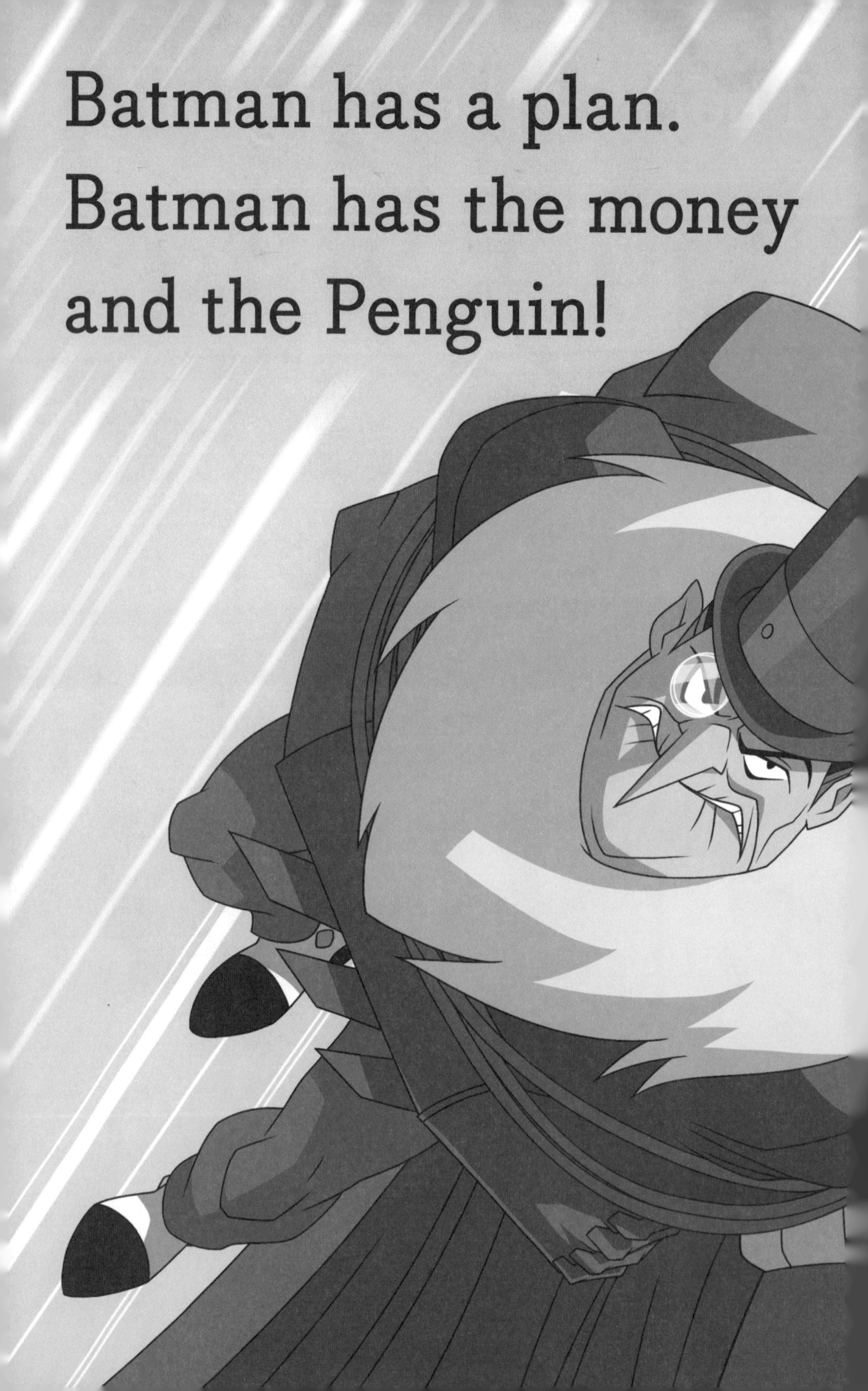

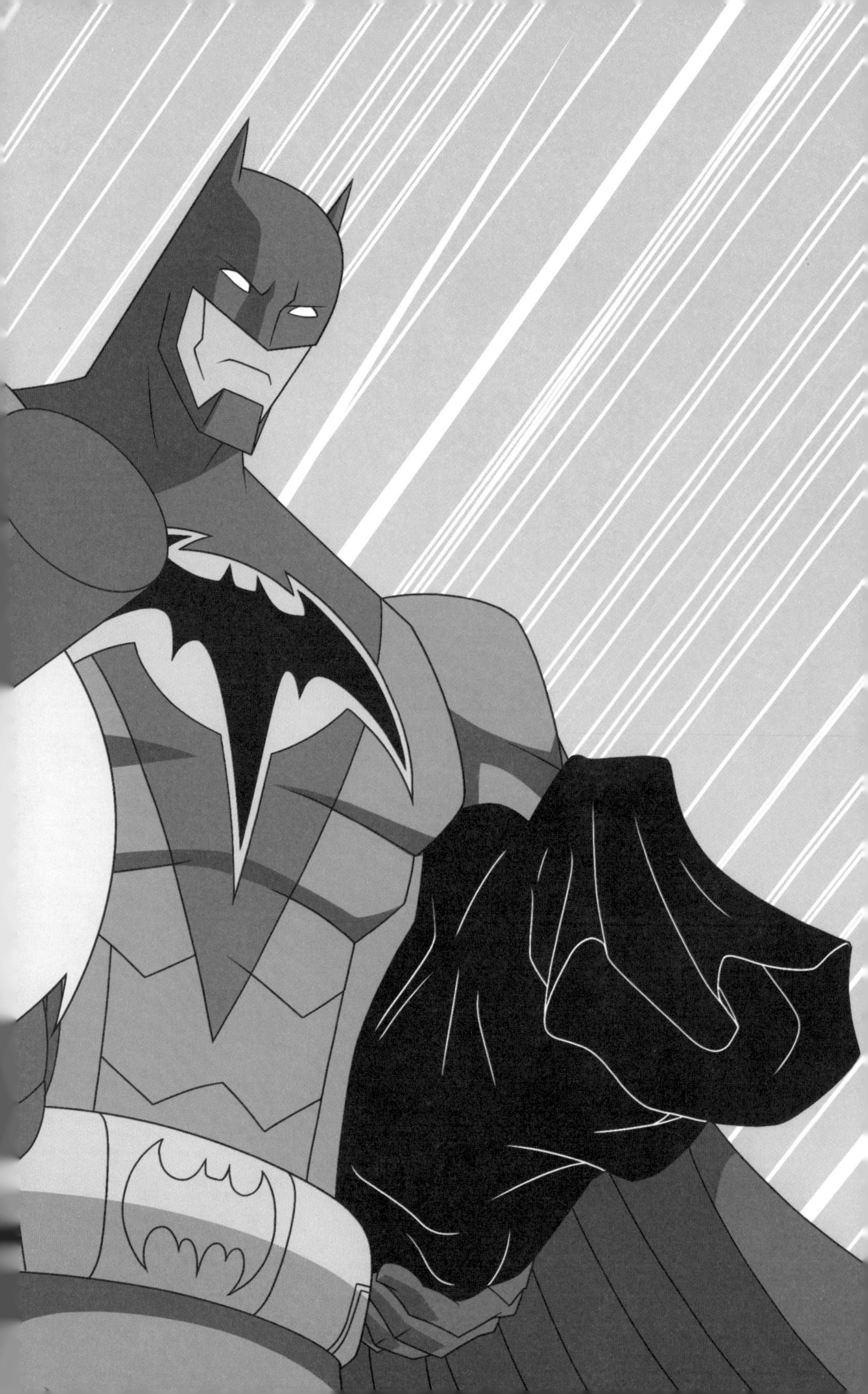

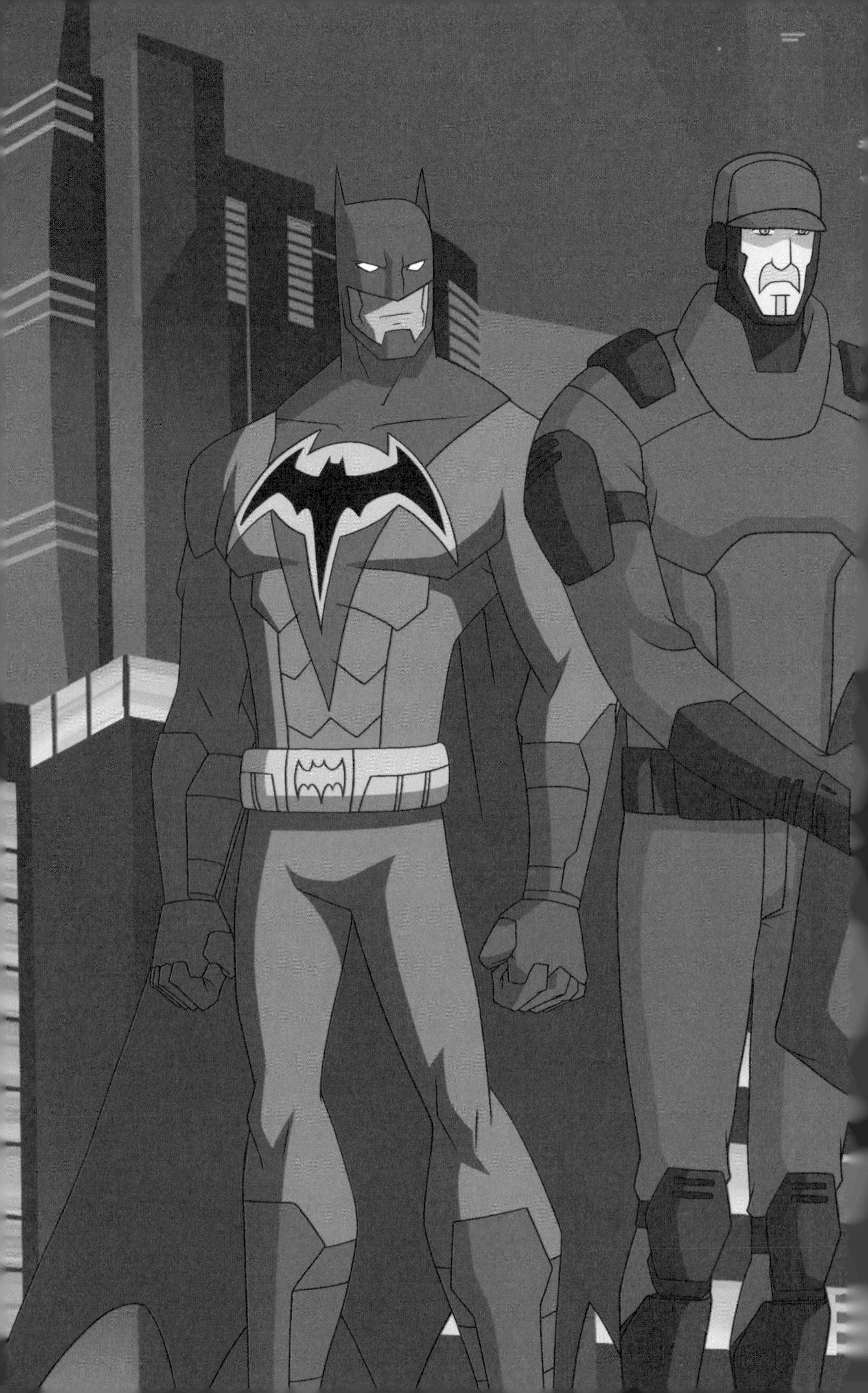

The Penguin is mad.

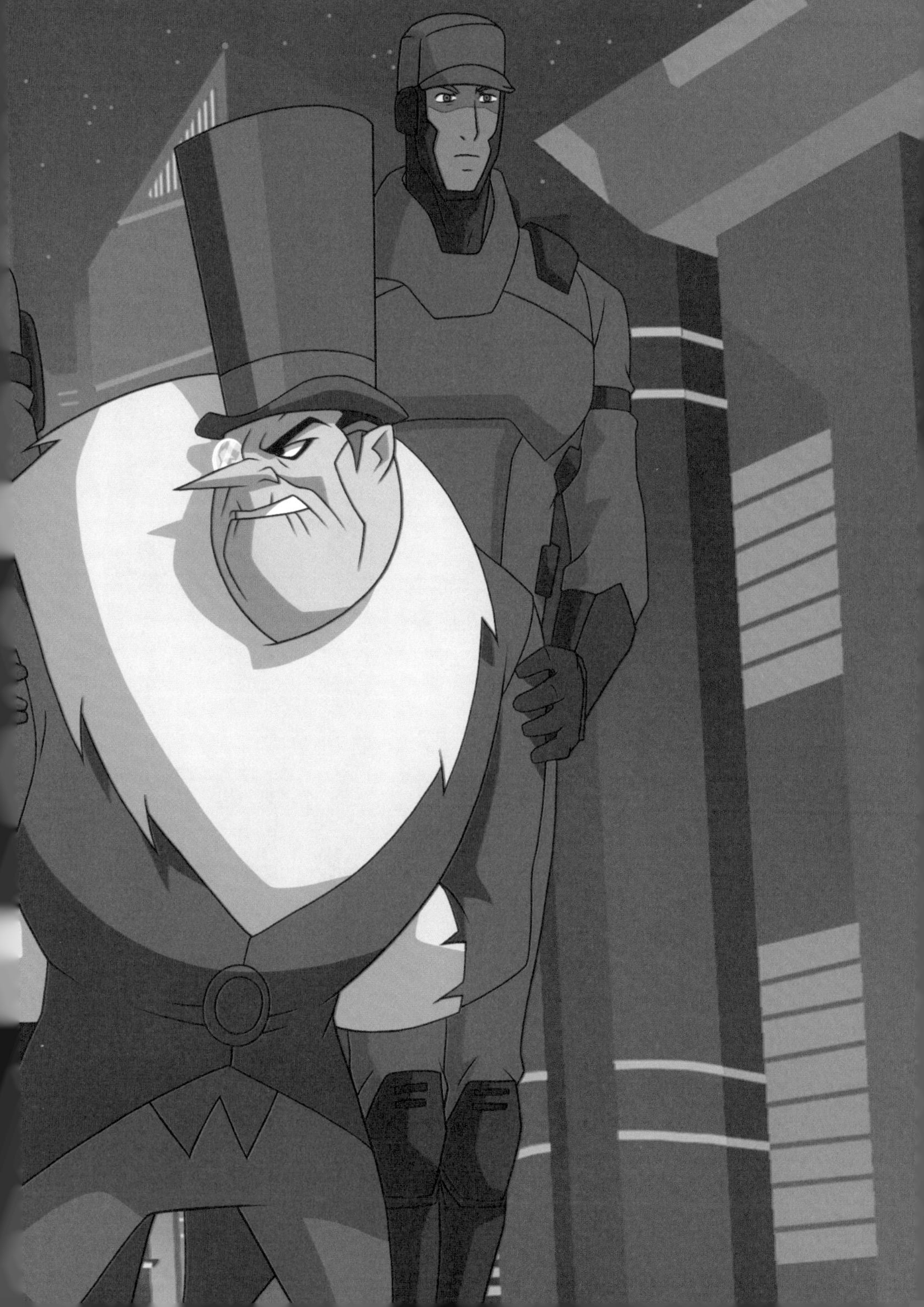

Everyone is glad.

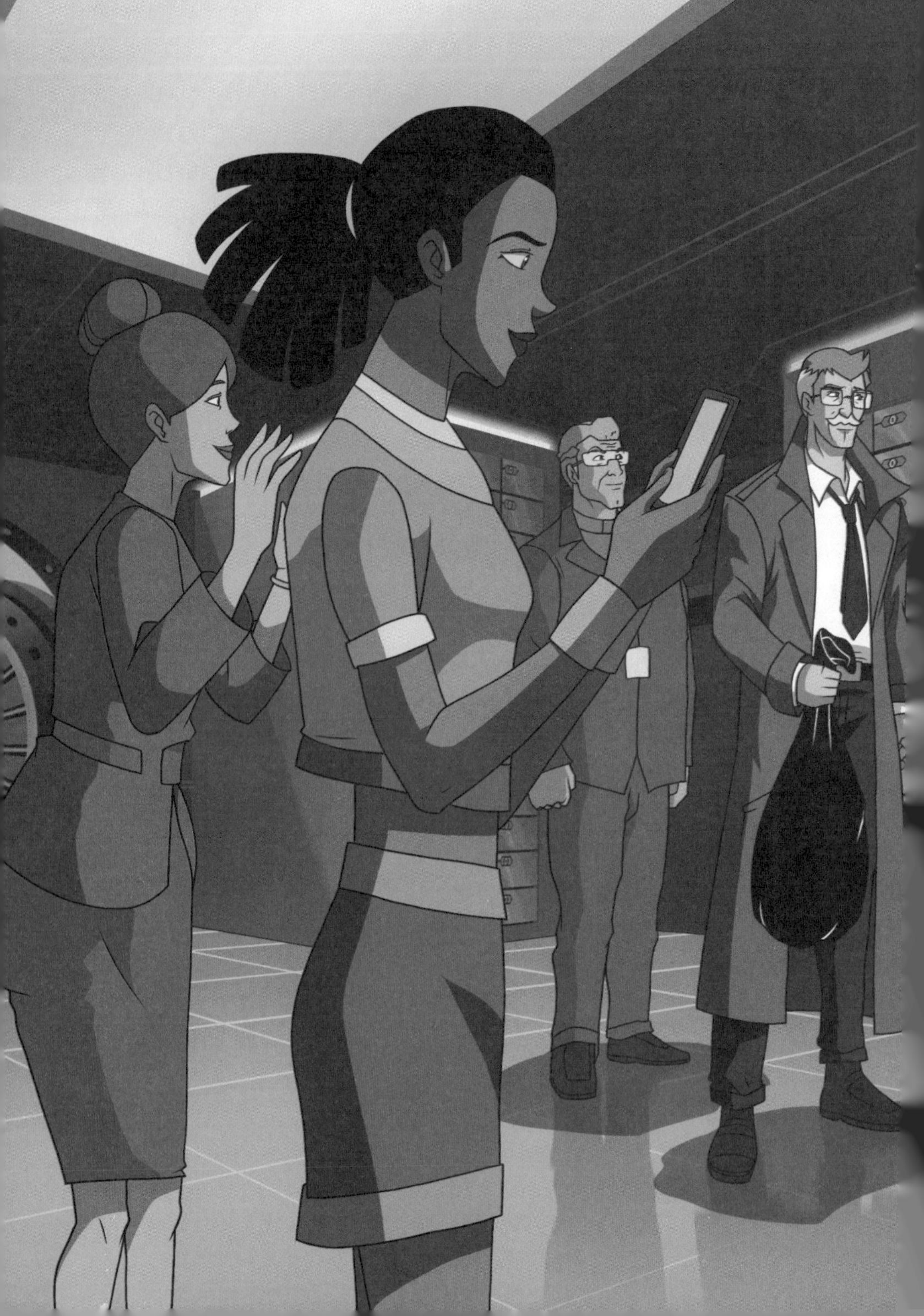

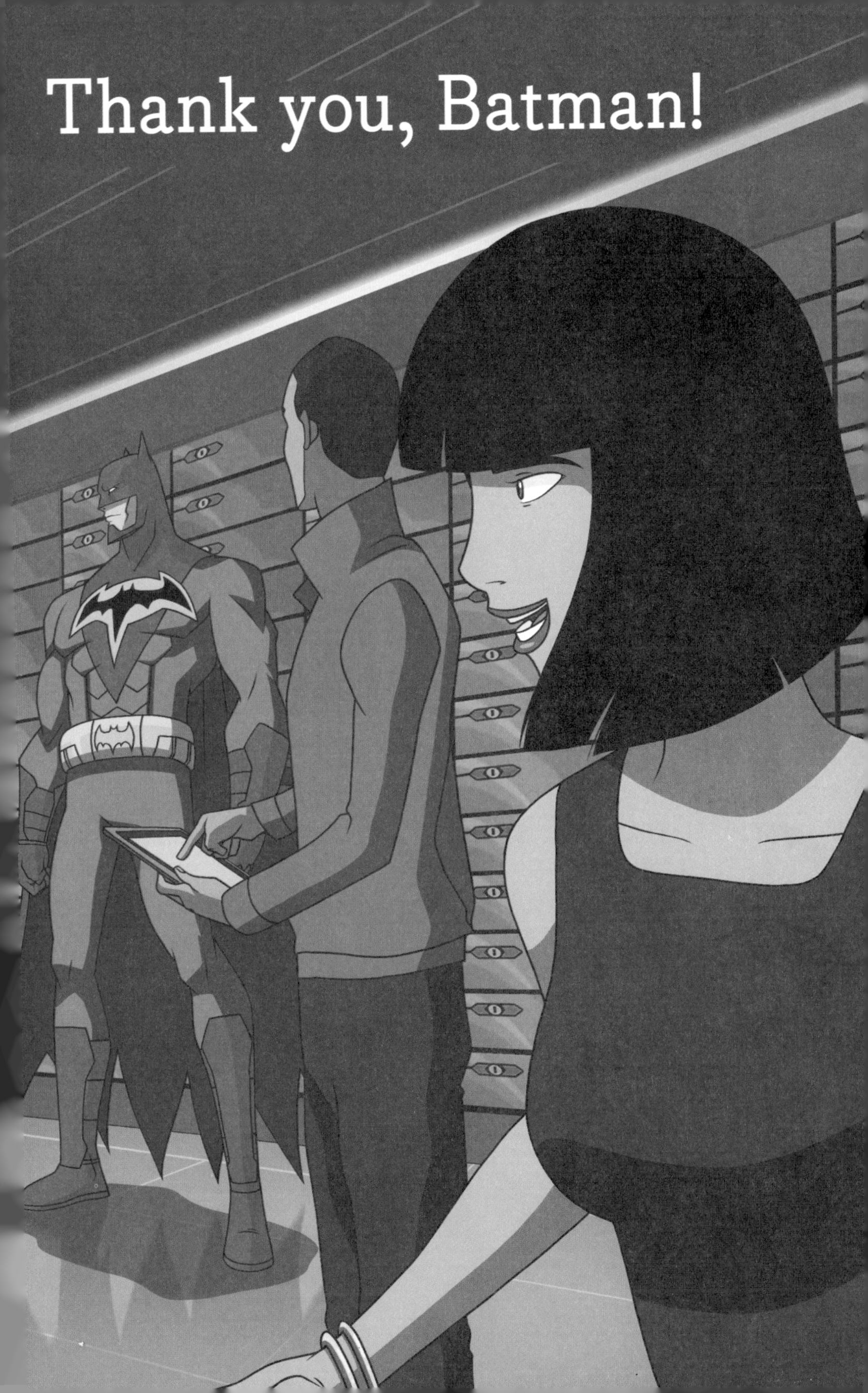
Thank you, Batman!

Now that you have read the story, can you answer these questions?

1. At the end of the story, why is everyone glad?

2. How did Batman reach the roof?

3. In this story, you read the rhyming words "mad" and "glad." Can you think of other words that rhyme with "mad" and "glad"?

Great job!
You are a reading star!